God's Masterpiece

Free Educator, Music and Program
Packets to accompany this book:
LisaCaprelli.com/In-His-Image
or write lisa@lisacaprelli.com

Published by Happy & Fun Lifestyle LLC
Author: Lisa Caprelli
Illustrator: Davey Villalobos

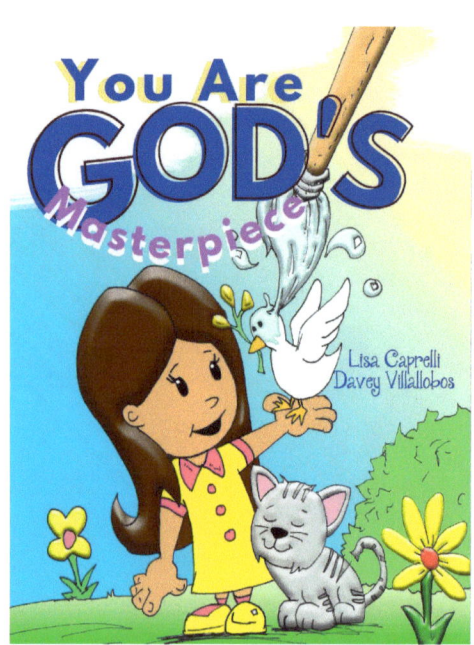

1st Edition **2023**
Filed with the Library of Congress Control
Publisher's Cataloging in Publication Data:
Author: Caprelli, Lisa;
Illustrator: Villalobos, Davey
Co-creator: Vasquez, Matthew
Series Name: In His Image

Paperback ISBN: 978-1-951203-32-0
Hardcover ISBN: 978-1-951203-34-4

This Book Belongs To:

Meet Joy. Learn about love from a Bible story.

Love is patient.

It does not envy.

It is not easily angered.

Love rejoices in the truth.

protects.

Love always trusts.

Love never fails.

Discussion Words

Patient

Kind

Envy

Boast

Proud

Dishonor

Self-Seeking

Angered

Wrongs

Rejoices

Truth

Protects

Trusts

Hopes

Perseveres

Always

Fails

Love

Dedication

To my sisters, mother and family for teaching me to how to find God's purpose:

Esperanza, Debbie, Suzanne, Ruth, Ginger, Rochelle, Claudia, Jasmine. Mandy, Alyssa, Andrew, Mike, Matt, Lori & Trey, and a beautiful army of Christian friends & family!

To an amazing illustrator, Davey: you have helped create beauty with imagination for children. Thank you ALL!

Lisa Caprelli

Lisa Caprelli is an elementary school speaker and creator of the Unicorn Jazz™ book and song series. She is a Christian writer and podcaster who believes in teaching the importance of love and belonging.

She loves visiting schools!
Write her at lisa@lisacaprell.com
or text: 949-677-8288